The
Terror of Mapooly
Moses Solomon

The Terror of Mapooly
© 2013 by Alexander F. Lee

cover illustration by Dana Henderson
© 2013 by Dana Henderson
All Rights Reserved

ISBN 978-0-9894902-1-4
eISBN 978-0-9894902-3-8

Printed in the United States of America

greeted me with sharp salutes. Together, we mounted the steps to the command platform overlooking the operations deck, where my eye caught the chaotic mess of ships filling the wraparound viewer that surrounded the bridge on three sides. Below our position, General Mapooly's dreadnoughts descended through the atmosphere while scores of landing craft emptied from both sides of the many troop carriers. As Mapooly's ships invaded, tiny vessels of all shapes and sizes—hundreds, perhaps thousands, of private craft—fled the planet in all directions. It was total pandemonium, a frenzied abandonment by those who could, while Mapooly's followers streamed in.

Captain Pavon met Admiral Kearn and myself on the command platform. "Sir, we have received a request for identification."

I smiled at Kearn. We could have said we were rejoining the People's Army, yet again. But why? "Let's see if we can slip in." I turned to Pavon. "Tell them our comm unit is damaged. Toss them a couple bursts of static."

Kearn gave Pavon a knowing nod. "Order the other ships to hold position out of detection range, Captain, and then take us down to the capital. Let's land somewhere outside the dome. Maybe the Agrian Fields, if it's not already taken."

"Yes, sir," Pavon said, departing to relay the order to the crew.

rifle—ironically, something far more ancient than the *rypniblade*.

"Lord Walmsley." It was Admiral Flan Kearn, my fleet commander, on the speaker. "We're approaching Pharry, and it's chaotic as hell in the atmosphere. Are you sure we should proceed?"

I drew in a determined breath. It was time. After Ostarand had conquered the majority of Eurania, Mapooly emerged from the far reaches of the star cluster with his Belaanian army. He defeated Ostarand in a head-to-head confrontation, drove the Revolutionary Guard across Eurania during a year-long campaign, and laid siege to Ostarand's home planet of Pharry. Two days ago, we intercepted signals that the month-long siege had finally broken through. The fighting had moved planetside.

I had to see the final outcome for myself, with my own eyes. This could be the end of the war. Would Mapooly emerge victorious and end the killing? Twenty-six long years—my entire adult career—and that following six centuries of outside occupation and disorder. Could we Euranians finally achieve a stable, lasting peace?

I reached for the channeling barrel. I always preferred the double barrel to the single.

"Hold position, Admiral. I'm on my way." I snapped the barrel into place and hung it next to the *rypniblade*, ready for use, before departing for the bridge.

Admiral Kearn and three of his assistants

For Mrs. Jensen,
Who Taught Me the Love of Mythology

My sincere thanks go to my editor, Mason McCann Smith, who kept pushing me to make the story better; Dana Henderson, for his inspiring cover image; and Suzy Vitello, for her insightful comments.

Additional thanks go to Curtis Chen, Steve Malick, Michael Stack, and Steven Wallace for all the helpful feedback.

Prologue

I never imagined that a civilian name could rise above those of the greatest military leaders of the Galactic Revolutions. Nor that all mention of this person's singular role in the outcome of the war would be deleted from the official accounts—by his own hand.

As we approached what I anticipated to be the concluding battle of the conflict that had engulfed the Euranian star cluster for over two decades, my mind was on logistics. Specifically, the men and women of the Greyban Corps under my command, their weapons, whether we could maneuver our way in, and what we might find when we landed.

I couldn't help but glance at my *rypniblade*, hanging on the wall in its plain gray, metal-lined sheath. The three-foot-long weapon still fulfilled a vital purpose: when the charge-guns petered out, you could still fight the old-fashioned way. But for me, it was more time-honored tradition and decoration than practical armament. I gave my rifle's transformer a final puff of the cleaning blower and proceeded to reassemble it. There was one catch about modern energy weapons. Though obviously built for the dirtiness of war, you never knew when static discharge, excessive grit, or a random spray of oil would render the finicky circuitry dead.

Acquiring a supply of these rifles for my men was something I was very proud of. The Greyban Corps was a small militia with modest manufacturing capabilities—mainly small firearms and explosives—and we relied on the regular armies for larger weaponry. Both Rai Ostarand's Revolutionary Guard and the People's Army of General e'Thuq Mapooly manufactured charge-pak weapons for their own use. By taking on a succession of jobs—small, local maneuvers—for first Ostarand and then Mapooly, and bargaining advanced arms for lesser pay, we received enough state-of-the-art weapons to remain a viable force as other contingents fell by the wayside.

In time, both armies effectively swept aside the majority of the regional warring factions, from small militias to large regular armies. Eventually, the Revolutionary Guard and the People's Army emerged as the final two combatants.

Of course, I had no idea that I might come upon something far more powerful than the charge-pak

1. *Curse of the Condemned*

As we landed, I saw colossal flames covering the mountaintop forests surrounding the domed capital of Seon. Pharry, the once-proud civilization that had emerged relatively unscathed from centuries of occupation, now descended into the depths of anarchy and self-consummation. On planet after planet, Ostarand and the Revolutionary Council had let flames burn and blood flow in their quest to eliminate enemy sympathizers, real or imagined, throughout Eurania. By the time Mapooly and his followers from Belaan launched their counteroffensive, Ostarand's deeds had left a trail of dead and dying that topped even the six hundred years of occupation.

We were not sad to hear of the bloodthirsty Ostarand's capture by Mapooly. At the same time, we were not relishing the thought of summoning our energy to combat the tyrant that Mapooly had become during his campaigns. The Greyban Corps had nowhere near the size or firepower of Mapooly's People's Army. We did not have ships that could defeat the Belaanian dreadnoughts in head-to-head engagement. Instead, we had to rely on stealth and the use of selective surgical strikes. In some ways, size became Mapooly's vulnerability. As his triumphs mounted, he lost his sharp edge, relying more on overwhelming brute force than on strategy or cunning. Our biggest advantage turned out to be the chaos that reigned everywhere. Whether in small ships or on foot, our small numbers could move everywhere with relative ease.

My men and I penetrated Seon as droves of civilians fled. Mapooly's armed forces and flocks of devoted followers from Mapooly's conquered worlds poured in. My troop commander, General Geo Genosser, and his hand-selected landing force accompanied me to the city center. We sneaked deep into the crowd, reaching a massive ornate fountain that dominated the classical-styled Pharrian square. Throngs had gathered to pelt rocks and hurl grievances at the white-clothed Ostarand. We were close enough to see his hands tied behind his back to one of the fountain legs, with an overhead placard that proclaimed "Traitor" in multiple dialects. After the Belaanian soldiers removed his hat to reveal an unkempt ring of silvery hair, they pointed their long *rypniblades* at him.

"Behold, your traitor!" Mapooly stepped

forward and presented Ostarand to the raucous crowd, his Pharrian pronunciations laced with a thick Belaanian accent. "What shall we do?"

"Burn him!" some cried.

"Decapitate him!" others yelled.

Ostarand's face twisted in defiance against the roar of the people. "Traitors!"

"Shall he live or shall he die?" Mapooly asked.

"Keep him alive!"

"Make him suffer!"

"Die, die, die!"

"You are all traitors!" Ostarand yelled, his voice barely audible above the screams of the crowd. "My army will wreak vengeance upon you all!"

General Genosser turned to me. "This is insane."

I knew Ostarand was as good as dead. My attention turned on Mapooly. He removed his combat helmet, revealing a mess of short-cropped black hair framing his large, pitch black eyes, stubby nose, and square jaw. He captivated the crowd like no other military leader I had known, his command presence rivaling that of the High Priest, Monseigneur Dhavail of Kelova. The Great Temple of Wiene had been the enduring beacon of the Euranian people during the dark age of occupation, a status far outweighing its nonexistent political or military influence. General Mapooly, meanwhile, now seemed victorious after capturing Ostarand. He raised his arms and basked in the attention of the people.

"Is Mr. Ostarand not a sad sight?" Mapooly turned to Ostarand. "You had the support of everyone who fought for Euranian independence and dreamed of freedom and self-rule. All who remembered the past—who dreamed of the golden age when the beacon of Etolis illuminated the galaxy—rose to stand at your side. You could have ruled a new Euranian dominion."

He turned back to the people. "He could have been the first ruler of a new empire!"

The crowd erupted. "Down with Ostarand!"

Mapooly turned back to Ostarand. "If only you had sought to govern, not to conquer."

"Choke on your words, *Shat'oq*!" Ostarand cursed. "You accuse me of conquering, yet you yourself are a conqueror!"

"I am a liberator," Mapooly corrected, whipping his maroon cloak over his shoulder, "and a uniter of those who have been liberated. There is a difference."

"There is no difference," Ostarand countered. "We both kill the enemy, even if they be our own people. We are two of a kind."

Mapooly turned to the crowd. "Are we two of a kind? Are Mr. Ostarand and I the same?"

"No! No! No!"

Mapooly smiled at Ostarand. He unsheathed his *rypniblade* with his right hand, drew his pistol with his left, and turned to the people. "What shall it be?

The blade or the blast?"

The crowd descended into utter pandemonium, some calling for the blast gun, but more for the *rypniblade*. We found ourselves surrounded by a mob delirium I'd never witnessed before. The blade faction began chanting, and as more joined in, the volume grew until it dominated the blast supporters into submission. I watched Ostarand look about in fury like a caged animal with nowhere to turn to. Mapooly's smile felt eerie, like that of a murderer premeditating a killing.

"I, for one, will be glad to be rid of Ostarand," Genosser said.

"Yes," I said, "but...."

I did not like the feel of General Mapooly. Though I had once paid Belaan a brief visit, we knew very little about the Belaanian people, their culture, or their temperament. Standing there, staring at their leader, I felt nervous. His facial expression was raw, vicious, almost bestial. Ostarand's fidgeting seemed to convey that he felt the same, that his end was imminent.

"The blade!" the mob chanted. "The blade! The blade!"

"The people have spoken," Mapooly said, "and so it is."

Ostarand's eyes bulged. "No!" He bared his teeth at Mapooly. "Mark my words! You are a demon from Luzomi's Hell and you will be cursed to walk the void of existence at Luzomi's pleasure, the undead of the eternal night, the bane of the human race."

Mapooly eyed his victim as Ostarand cursed. He took a step away and, with a lightning whirl, backhanded the *rypniblade* across Ostarand's neck, drawing a gush of blood and slicing through flesh and bone. The crowd roared its approval, their arms held high in the air. I saw Ostarand's head fly off with an outpouring of blood and bounce away as his body collapsed at Mapooly's feet.

At that instant, I could not help but wonder about my fellow Euranians.

"Here we go, Geo," I said to Genosser. I felt tired. I had been fighting battles my entire adult life and now it seemed that yet another phase of combat was beginning. "I've seen enough. The fighting has turned again. We'd better pass through the crowd, while we can."

We scrambled back through the mob, out to our ship. Once aboard, we took off and flew through the maze of inbound and outbound traffic before departing for deep space.

"Sir, you've been tight-lipped since we departed Pharry. What really did you see?" Petra Trophet, my Chief of Staff, sat across my desk, reviewing status reports on her digi-com.

It had been nearly a week. We were cruising through space, circling between Kelova and Bexel. This gave us the flexibility to reach any of the major

core planets on short notice. Still struggling to break everything down in my mind, I relaxed my fists, resting them on my plain, empty desktop. I leaned back in my high-back chair and found myself wishing I had decorated my office. Paintings, plants, anything therapeutic. "It was ugly."

"Ostarand?" Trophet asked, her thick eyebrows raised with curiosity. "Or Mapooly?"

I felt like dismissing the question. "Ostarand lost his head." It wasn't the flying body part that bothered me. After two decades of bloody carnage, I had witnessed plenty of flailing body parts, both with and without blood, and with and without death screams. No, it was the memories of the living— Ostarand's caged desperation, Mapooly's bestial snarl, and the mindless delirium of the mob—that gnawed at me. There was something disturbing. I could still feel a tightness in my stomach.

After a long pause, I gave Trophet a sorry smile before finally giving her an answer. "I don't like the way General Mapooly looked. He's a born killer, plain and simple."

"Hmm." Trophet rubbed her dimpled chin with her hand. "There's been chatter in the ranks, sir. The men are wondering what will happen to them, now that the People's Army is emerging victorious. Will the Greyban Corps remain active? If not, will we be assisting the men with the transition back home?" She put her digi-com on the desk and folded her arms. "Lord Walmsley, what do you think life will be like under General Mapooly?"

It was a good question. I had hoped things would point toward reconstruction. War had wreaked havoc on every major planet in Eurania, with many old governments toppled and tossed aside by one campaign or another. Agreement on a New Order would take a lot of hard work by all parties. "At this point, Petra, I really don't know."

I tried to convince myself that it wasn't just about Mapooly, but I knew better. Eventually, leaders from the core worlds would come forth, once they had gained control of their planets from the many contenders vying for local power. But for now, for the Euranian star cluster, the strongest would command. That was General Mapooly, the Belaanian People's Army, and his many followers.

I made my decision. "We're not disbanding. Not yet." I stood up. "We may be small, but until we know that there will be a real, sustainable peace under General Mapooly, all cells of the Greyban Corps will remain on active status."

"Understood." Trophet bowed. "I will relay the message, sir."

I watched Trophet depart my office with the feeling that I had made the right stand. But, I did not feel good about it. The men and women of the Greyban Corps deserved better than to be kept on edge with no specific objectives.

I sat back down and took my digi-com from the desk drawer. I needed to leave myself a note to

discuss the future of the Corps with Trophet, Genosser, and Kearn. Would it be safe to send the men back to their homes? How would we know? I switched the flatscreen digi-com on. My father's smiling face greeted me. Though a forty-year-old portrait, a warm feeling of old still resonated as fresh as when I was small. Happiness and admiration. And the familiar hollow pain that never went away.

It had been over five years since my father died in battle. The Greyban Corps originally formed after his call throughout Alscras to organize in the face of impending incursions from neighboring factions. Of the major core worlds of Eurania, Alscras had the scrappiest history, one centered more on the individual initiatives of local power brokers than the on-again, off-again monarchy. My father took us to the stars with as many like-minded comrades as he could reach. Our first ships were overhauled salvage jobs, but as long as the star-drives worked, the ships were put to use.

With each job the Corps performed for successively larger armies, we reaped rewards: money, of course, but also arms and faster, better-equipped ships. From my father, I learned the value of picking and choosing, of patience, and of striking with everything you had. By shooting to kill, I became an able-bodied, successful soldier on the battlefield.

The Corps slowly grew after several campaigns.

A satellite cell formed on nearby Bexel. Surprisingly, a third, very small unit organized on Onglus. That far-distant planet had always held an unusual attraction to me. I could be a good self-styled soldier like my father, but the fighting exhausted me. The constant back-and-forth travel grew repetitive. Deep down, I wanted a different direction, something that could fulfill a lifetime better than the endless journeying from one planet to another, one battlefield to another. Something elusive that I could not identify.

Then, my father was killed and I had to pull our units out of a major military disaster. Once we reassembled, I had to address the decimated morale throughout our ranks. I knew the best remedy—the best way to hold everyone together—would be a quick success, so we took on another campaign. It was a high-risk offensive against yet another of the countless local chieftains. I could barely keep our combined forces coordinated during battle, and we suffered tremendous casualties. But in the end, we outlasted our opponents in a bloody battle of attrition. By emerging from the skirmish victorious, the Greyban Corps was saved. Though I barely knew what I was doing, I was the new leader.

Now, with the war nearly over, I needed a fresh perspective, different from those of my subordinates. Was now the time to turn my attention to a possible new direction, both for myself and for the men and women of the Corps? Would General

Mapooly want to bring Onglus under his rule or did he already have enough territory to deal with? I quickly entered these questions into the digi-com as a reminder to myself.

As I finished, Trophet buzzed in.

"Lord Walmsley, we've intercepted a signal from Kelova." My Chief of Staff sounded urgent. "General Mapooly's forces have appeared without warning."

My muscles tensed.

"The High Priest has been taken away."

I wasn't sure I heard right. "The High Priest of the Great Temple?" I had to ask, to be sure. The Temple of Wiene was the official seat of the High Priest of Lord Oscanos and Mother Gheriah. Though the planet Kelova was centrally located, the High Priest offered no strategic or military value. However, untold numbers throughout Eurania heeded his centuries-old—perhaps millenia-old— dogmatic, ritualistic teachings. Perhaps Mapooly wanted the High Priest to voice support for Belaanian rule over the central worlds. No, that didn't feel right. My instinctive reaction to this unusual move by Mapooly was guarded and pessimistic. I still remembered the General's visage at Ostarand's execution.

"Yes, sir. From the wording in the message, he was seized by force."

The most powerful military conqueror capturing a pacifist preacher could not be a good sign. I wasn't too terribly devoted to the old Temple rituals, but General Mapooly was up to something and I had to find out what it was—for our own survival, as well as the High Priest's.

"Call Admiral Kearn and General Genosser in, Petra. We need to talk about this."

"Opinions?" I looked from Genosser to Kearn to Trophet, each seated across my desk.

After hearing my feelings about General Mapooly, each member of my inner circle showed a contemplative look on his or her face. At this point, we were relatively anonymous, a small fighting force that posed no threat to the Belaanian army. Things would change if we attempted to rescue the High Priest—we would be in open opposition to Mapooly, an idea I figured no one would relish.

Genosser, the eldest of the three, took a deep inhale from the stub of his *cuira* stick and blew the smoke out to the side. Trophet pursed her lips, her customary disapproval of the earthy aroma. I switched up the ventilation.

"At this point," Genosser said, "we have no target, no information about our opposition, and no understanding of what the consequences of failure would be. The Belaanian Army has been unstoppable. We might need the protection of another regular army." He took another puff. "We need those answers before we can seriously consider a rescue mission."

Genosser's response typified his approach. Details first, then decision. I turned to Kearn, younger than Genosser by a decade, but significantly grayer from the burden of command without the stress-relieving benefit of face-to-face combat.

"I advise caution," Kearn said in his usual matter-of-fact tone. "We are entering a new paradigm, one we are unfamiliar with. With the fighting all but over, we need to figure out whether our current deployments are still appropriate."

Trophet fidgeted in her chair. She didn't seem to like either man's response. Both Genosser and Kearn had voiced important points. I was curious to hear her thoughts.

Kearn faced Trophet. "I would hate to send a task force on a mission before we've figured out if they'd be needed in a more-vital position."

Genosser blew out another breath.

Both of my military leaders were consistently predictable. They commanded the means to achieve victory, but were averse to losses. Their caution had been a key factor in the Greyban Corps' longevity. But it didn't seem likely to me that we would be able to attain the level of certainty that Genosser and Kearn wanted. The longer we waited, the less likely the High Priest would still be alive.

"Lord Walmsley." Trophet wasted no time. "We need to liberate the High Priest. I don't need to remind you of our blood oath."

"No, you don't." I glanced at Genosser and Kearn.

Starting with my father's earliest followers, every person had sworn allegiance on the blood of their right forearm with the words, "To My God, My Sovereign, and My Comrades," before joining. It was a simple oath that focused the mission of the Greyban Corps.

It also gave a very pure, almost naive view of the high clergy. Over the centuries, the Temple of Wiene had somehow survived repeated invasions of Kelova. The devoted believed this to be by the hand of the Almighty. To me, however, nothing was so simple. It smelled of a pattern of compromise with the conquerors, a convenient corruption of the ministry, practical, but a betrayal at the feet of the sanctuary gods.

I had other misgivings about a search for Monseigneur Dhavail. Of what real value was a priest, influential as he was, when dealing with the most powerful military since the heyday of the ancient Etolian empire?

"I'm not disputing our overall mission," Genosser pointed out. "I'm saying we have no target to aim for."

"Nor do we know how long we would be occupied with an undertaking such as this," Kearn added.

"The believers among our ranks would never forgive us if we failed to even attempt a rescue,"

Trophet said. "There are a lot of followers of the Great Temple, and their spiritual leader's life is on the line. The credibility of our motto is what faces us."

"We may suffer avoidable losses on an ill-conceived attempt," Genosser said.

"And we may suffer even more avoidable losses from desertion," Trophet countered.

All eyes turned to me. Trophet had earlier pointed out the many unanswered questions among the ranks to me. I couldn't deny the importance of upholding the oath. The loyalty of the Corps could depend on it.

There was one other question that seemed even more important to me. "What purpose does Mapooly have in seizing the High Priest?" Above all, my overriding concern was Mapooly. "If we could rescue Monseigneur Dhavail, we would gain a unique opportunity to learn about the Belaanian leader from the High Priest."

Trophet nodded.

Kearn folded his hands together under his chin. "Interesting."

My mind was made up. "Let's find out." I leaned forward in my seat and said to Kearn, "It might help us figure out our new posture. Agreed?"

Trophet answered first. "Agreed."

Kearn bowed his head for a moment, then nodded. "It might prove to be a good move."

Genosser crumpled up his spent *cuira* stick,

tossed it into the disposal in the corner of the desk, and reached into his pocket for a new stick. "We're assuming that the High Priest is still alive. We still have no target."

"Mapooly has to have a purpose for capturing him, instead of killing him," I said, rising. "Contact the other cells and have them gather intelligence on Mapooly's past movements. Has he tended to repeatedly use certain prison facilities?"

Genosser lit his stick and took a deep inhale. "We're on it, sir." He, Kearn, and Trophet stood and saluted, and I dismissed them, still harboring silent doubts about our new undertaking.

The cells moved swiftly, sending in their various findings in a matter of days. Soon, Trophet called Genosser and Kearn back to my office to present to me the summary of their analysis: "We find, sir, that he has mostly used three locations: Planet K, Acromis, and Minoss."

"Acromis is very large in both scale and population," Kearn said. "The prisoners are kept in large, open-air pens and monitored from armed watchtowers. With no individual confinement, it's not possible to hide someone prominent."

Genosser nodded. "Planet K is a large planet, and the penal facility is surrounded by native settlements. There would be too much risk of someone accidentally seeing the High Priest under guard. Minoss is the most distant, and the most isolated. It's deep inside a planetoid, one of millions in the Lorium asteroid belt. If I were General Mapooly, the choice would seem clear—assuming the Monseigneur is not being held on Belaan, of course."

"I agree with General Genosser," Trophet said.

"I also agree," Kearn said.

Fighting on unconventional terms had become second nature to all of us. But facing the possible conclusion of those days, the rescue of the High Priest seemed a different venture. I had a responsibility to question myself. Was the reward worth the risk of taking a task force so far out of range? Kearn's caution about being caught out of position hadn't been addressed. Neither had Genosser's point about the possibility of the High Priest being held on Belaan. Also, I still had my own question of whether Dhavail was truly a spiritual leader worth rescuing, or only the latest in a long line of mouthpieces presiding over a millenia-old institution.

But then, the memories of Mapooly on Pharry flashed into my mind. We had to find out what sort of person we were facing. I was certain of that much.

"Very well," I said. "Minoss it is. Please begin preparing mission plans."

An unexpected breakthrough came in the form of Whinn Rexold, a maintenance technician from

Bexel. She had served in a similar maintenance tech capacity at the Minoss prison during the first decade of the war before a devastating attack by the Revolutionary Guard destroyed her home and family on Bexel. Deserting Minoss, the heartbroken Rexold fled to the newly-formed Bexelian cell of the Greyban Corps, a unit she eventually joined, though she was not a fighting woman.

Communicating by scrambled carrier signal from a Bexelian transport that was cruising at a secret location, Rexold described to Genosser and myself what she could recall of the Minoss security setup.

"I am sure many upgrades have been made since my departure, sir."

Even sitting alone in my office, with no other noises from the rest of the ship, Rexold's scrambled-and-unscrambled voice barely stood out from the signal's background static.

"But given its remote location, I would not expect any major changes to the backbone structure of the facility."

"Understood," Genosser said. "Describe the backbone to us."

"Four spokes converge to a common centerpoint. These are the four redundant energy sources which power the central unit. The configuration of the underground prison facility itself is also made up of a central station and four wings, each with a surface entrance module at the terminal point. There are also bypass tunnels between the wings, which may be helpful. From the central control unit, a surveillance network radiates out to the four wings. Exterior surveillance is separate, though, powered by remote onsite sources, not the central unit."

Genosser and I exchanged glances. The interior system could be taken out at the central hub. But the exterior would need a blanket effect to disrupt all the remote sources at the same time.

I reached for the speaker. "Ms. Rexold, were there any previous attempts to knock out the security systems, to your knowledge?"

There was a long pause filled with static. "I believe that the last attempt was several years before the exterior system was changed to remote power. The change may have been a result of that attempt."

Genosser asked, "Can you describe the bypass tunnels?"

"They're irregular, sir."

Genosser frowned. "Do you mean the locations or the size of the tunnels?"

"Both, sir. They're not systematic. They were meant to connect together pairs of specific locations, like a parts supply with a corresponding usage location. But since so many were built, many either interconnect or end close to the start of another. I'm afraid it would be difficult to describe the layout."

I turned to Genosser. "We're going to need to use these tunnels. Do you know how you want to approach this?"

Genosser hit the mute switch. "We're going to need Rexold to be our guide."

I was afraid he was going to say that. It was always risky to use an untested person on a first mission. How Rexold would perform in a life-and-death situation was anybody's guess.

I turned the speaker back on. "That will be all for now, Ms. Rexold. Thank you."

Genosser rose as I switched off the speaker. "I don't think it's a good idea to go in blindly, but I'll get my men working on a plan."

"Geo...." I held up my hand.

Genosser stopped at the door, awaiting my order.

"Go ahead and bring Rexold in." I had never met the woman. It seemed a reasonable step to assess her capabilities. The viability of the mission could depend on it.

"Whinn Rexold, Senior Maintenance Technician A-3." Rexold took a step into my office and bowed. She was short, the top of her head level with Genosser's shoulder, with small eyes, a dark complexion, and short-cropped hair dyed bright blue.

"Welcome, Ms. Rexold." I took my seat behind my desk and motioned for Rexold and Genosser to sit in the two chairs before me. Glancing at Rexold's file on my digi-com display, I said, "Your performance record with the Bexelian cell is outstanding." I scrolled through the record to confirm that I had not overlooked anything. "Have you ever been sent into the field?"

"I'm not a soldier, sir."

I held up my hand to relax her. "I didn't mean combat. Maybe as support personnel for impromptu mop-up work? Something that's not detailed in the record?"

After thinking for a moment, she said, "I once helped restart a set of dynamos on Eeras, after the Revolutionary Guard had departed. That was about five years ago."

That was what I was looking for. "So you worked with military personnel on that occasion?"

"There were only a handful of us civilian technicians. Most of the work was done by the soldiers." She shrugged her shoulders. "Maybe that's why my involvement wasn't documented."

I glanced at Genosser, who had quietly lit a *cuira* stick. It was time to pose the question. Rexold's experience was minimal at best, but not nonexistent.

"Ms. Rexold, you may be the best person for an upcoming mission."

Her eyes bulged. "Me, sir? I don't think so." She shook her head vehemently. "The work on Eeras was a long time ago and it was a very, very small job. I haven't been assigned to a mission since."

"Relax, Ms. Rexold," Genosser said between puffs.

Rexold took a deep breath. "Yes, sir. Maybe it's not a combat mission."

I didn't know whether to smile or grimace. Either way, I suppressed it. Her reaction was understandable. Her only previous experience with the war was a horrific one—the discovery of the bombed-out remains of her home and the painful aftermath of burying her family. I had to determine if she was strong enough to put those memories aside for a higher cause.

"If I told you what the mission was about, that would leave you with the choice of participating— or being sequestered until it was over."

She shook her head again. "I can't imagine choosing to participate."

"It's important," I said with a firm voice.

Silence filled the room. Her hands began to tremble. She spoke quietly but quickly. "It's Minoss, isn't it? That's why you were asking me about it." I saw in her eyes that her mind was racing. "You want me to accompany a team there...to spring someone?"

"Perhaps." I didn't want to lock her into a decision, yet. She needed time to digest her line of thought. But I was impressed by her conduct under the pressure.

"Oh God." She closed her eyes, ran her hands through her hair, and let out a desperate sigh. "Why me?"

"It would make sense," Genosser said. "You know the facility. You would be surrounded by our soldiers, and it must be someone important to warrant such a long journey."

She opened her eyes with a look that wavered between fear and distress. "Who?"

That was the question I needed to hear. "The High Priest, Monseigneur Dhavail."

Rexold's jaw dropped. I feared that she might pass out. But as she held steady, the look in her eyes seemed to change.

Her service record held multiple comments noting her strong devotion to the worship of the Euranian Ancestors, the pantheon of deities who created the universe and the human race. Rexold was one of the multitude of followers of the Great Temple who would lay down their life for the High Priest. For someone like her, the Greyban oath to serve God, Crown, and her fellow Euranians should be reason enough to go on the mission. That was what I was betting on.

Rexold took a deep breath. Her trembling calmed. She looked straight at me. "I'll go."

The task force consisted of four ships: the lander, an escort, a comm craft equipped with a jammer, and a small refueler. I entered the cockpit of the lander to take in the view of the fleet, which was holding position near the border of the Outer Territories. Admiral Kearn had long ago given up his objections about my penchant for accompanying Genosser into the field. It had been my father's style of command, it had served me well, and for this mission, I needed to make first contact with Monseigneur Dhavail. The High Priest was that important.

"All ships are ready for departure." Genosser's voice came over the speaker from the comm craft.

"Begin communications black-out," Kearn replied from the flagship. "Good luck. Out."

The pilot shut off the speaker and steered the lander into position behind the comm craft and the escort. Behind me, two dozen hand-selected men and women sat in the hold, silent but alert. I could see, at the far end of one row of soldiers, Whinn Rexold in full combat armor with her infrared helmet visor raised, unmoving as a statue.

Returning my gaze to the front window, I could see the rest of the fleet drift away. In actuality, it was our four mission craft that were drifting away from the stationary fleet. The comm craft jumped into hyperspace, then the escort.

The pilot illuminated a green light on the console. "Ready, sir."

We were next, with the refueler following us. It would be a long journey to the far edge of the Outer Territories, where Minoss was situated, but after all the sitting around and pondering, it felt good to be back in action.

Several days later, we entered the Lorium Belt and quickly located Minoss, a dirty-gray, unremarkable asteroid among uncounted unremarkable asteroids. An isolated world in a remote location, Minoss had been left lightly guarded, without a single ship in orbit or on the surface. This was something we had hoped for. If Mapooly had positioned even a single capital warship to guard the asteroid, we would have had to abort the mission.

Our ship maneuvers were now running on preset programming, everything coordinated by the synchronized computers. The lander and its escort approached Minoss from the far side, out of detection of the prison, while the comm craft held position over a neighboring asteroid, H8365. The refueler remained safely outside the asteroid belt. As we skimmed over the surface of Minoss, ahead of the terminator line, the commandos activated their life-support gear, readied their weapons, and lined up in position to disembark. I stayed in the cockpit with the pilot, my rifle in my grasp, watching. Below the window, a small counter blinked.

The prison's surface modules—squat, metallic domes—came into view over the horizon. The counter flashed bright red and a jamming signal broadcast from the comm craft, momentarily cutting the prison's communications. At the same time, a high-frequency pulse fired from the escort ship, penetrating Minoss' surface and bathing the prison in a field of disruptive energy at the moment the sunlight hit.

With all systems—both the prison's and our ship's—now disabled, we glided down to the surface and landed, only a short distance away from the entrance module. The doors manually released and the Greyban commandos poured out. On the monitor, I watched my men overpower the two guards with blades only and a minimal amount of combat or commotion. After the older sentry was killed, the younger sentry surrendered. I then received the "all clear" from the squad leader, the signal for Rexold and I to disembark the lander. With Rexold as our "guide," we descended into the darkened subterranean levels of the facility. Along the way, I positioned my men to guard the route back to the surface. If all went well, we could be finished before the garrison was mobilized.

Despite not having set foot in Minoss for over a decade, Rexold managed to navigate the narrow maze of bypass tunnels, avoiding all the chaos and activity that no doubt engulfed the central station. Soon, she brought us to the High Priest, Monseigneur Dhavail, who sat disheveled in his stone cell in an oversized gray coverall and what looked like layers of dust and dirt.

"Who are you?" Dhavail blurted out, his arm

raised to shield his eyes from our lights.

I lowered my rifle and lifted my helmet visor so that he could see my face in full view. "Metiar Walmsley," I introduced myself, bowing, "and a squad from the Greyban Corps, at your service." I motioned to the door, and my men outside, with my rifle. "If you will come with us, we will escort you out of captivity."

The High Priest took a step backward, cowering into the corner of his cell. "I've never heard of you. Whose military do you report to?"

The harsh tone of the High Priest's voice—suggesting distrust, perhaps suspicion—was not what I had expected. If I didn't know better, I would have thought that the Monseigneur wanted to remain in captivity. "We're an independent militia, Your Holiness, committed to the service of the Euranian Ancestors, the crowns of Alscras and Bexel, and the defense of innocent civilians. We don't have much time, if you would please come with us." I stepped toward him.

A sharp whistle sounded from the mini-mic on my shoulder. Systems were coming back online, and enemy personnel had been sighted. "The guards are alerted to our presence." If the High Priest didn't comply, immediately, we would be engaged in a firefight. "We have to go!"

"Not with you!" Monseigneur Dhavail took another step back. "How do I know you're not part of a trap set by General Mapooly?"

"Please, Your Holiness!" It was Rexold, lifting her visor. "Believe in the mysterious ways of the Almighty."

The Monseigneur hesitated, seemingly undecided. I stepped in and grabbed his shoulder with a hard pull. The High Priest obediently followed me out. I pushed him ahead, hastening his pace into a brisk run through the lineup of men guarding our route back to the surface.

Except for the High Priest's unpredictable reaction, it had been one of the smoothest, most-successful operations we ever undertook. As we boarded the lander and took off, making good our escape, I could only hope that the Monseigneur would be useful, and not just a warm body we had picked up.

2. *The Unseen Realm*

"May the Almighty bless you and your brave men and women!" Monseigneur Dhavail accepted a cup of warm brewed Kelovan tea with both hands and a smile. After cleaning up in my temporary quarters on the escort, the High Priest looked noticeably more relaxed, though he still wore the same drab-gray, sack-like prisoner outfit. At least he was happy to be out of captivity. His shoulder-length hair was back to the familiar reddish-auburn, washed and combed. But with the dirt and grime washed off, his face now seemed a bit pale and lacking in a customary healthy pinkness. His cheeks were a touch gaunt, not the well-fed plumpness I remember from his wide-cast appearances. He hadn't been imprisoned for very long. I was surprised at how much weight he had lost and wondered if, under the many layers of his usual ceremonial garb, he might actually be a frail man.

"I've instructed the chief to prepare your food according to the temple guidelines."

Dhavail bowed. "That is very good."

"Please sit and relax." I dispensed a second cup of tea and motioned him to a pair of cushioned chairs to the side of my portable desk. "Perhaps we can discuss your experience."

The Monseigneur sat with a loud exhale and slumped for a second before assuming his normal, dignified posture. Though the brief slouch surprised me, I could forgive him a moment's loss of stately presence. But there was no time to lose—I finally had my opportunity to learn about Mapooly.

"Why do you think you were captured?"

High Priest Dhavail leaned forward in his chair. "I don't need to speculate. I know why I was captured." His eyes turned disturbingly dark. "Are you a believer, Lord Walmsley?"

I nodded. Like most parents, my father and mother had taught me the stories and beliefs of Lord Oscanos, Mother Gheriah, and the other Euranian Ancestors when I was small, stories that were repeated during my schooling.

The Monseigneur nodded with approval. "That is good. You will understand me when I say that we are on the verge of a spiritual crisis that Eurania has not seen in over a millenium."

A millenium would go back to the ancient Etolian empire. I was not aware of any "spiritual crises" during that era, the golden age of Eurania.

"Please explain." I took a sip of tea and focused on the details of the High Priest's account.

"I woke up to the blade-point of Mapooly," Dhavail began. "His men had infiltrated the Temple of Weine in the predawn hours. He said that I held the key to something he needed, which no one else could offer—a miracle from the Almighty Euranus."

"Interesting," I said. So, Mapooly did have a specific purpose in capturing Dhavail.

"Of course, I was scared," Dhavail said, "but I was able to summon strength from Lord Oscanos. I told Mapooly, 'The Creator of the universe does not answer to the point of a blade,' and he lowered his *rypniblade*. I asked him what was his issue, and he answered with one word: 'Beacheau.'"

I recognized the name, perhaps the only Belaanian name better known than Mapooly's: his wife's. She had been born with a terminal condition of the brain. The general sentiment in the media was that her ascension to adulthood was already a miracle.

"She was dying," Dhavail continued, "apparently past the point of medical treatment...." He paused and slowly shook his head in sadness. "I tried to reason with him. I told him that life and death are the way of things, that we all transition to the next life, where the Almighty reigns with the Euranian Ancestors, where disease and suffering such as his wife's are vanquished, where life prevails."

He was a High Priest now, reciting the overly familiar passages.

Dhavail's face contorted. "Mapooly would not accept this truth. He whipped out his *rypniblade* and snarled like a wild man. 'I am the liberator of our people, the uniter of our race. I will be the ruler of Eurania, and she will be my Queen.' Then he pointed the blade into my face. 'You must plead with the Almighty to spare her!' He dragged me out to his soldiers. Within the hour, I was en route to Belaan."

This was a side of Mapooly that I was not expecting. He was not intent on a military or territorial objective, but a personal one. I recalled my one visit to that far-off world of poisonous ammonia and methane cloud cover. I had learned that, in the distant past, the forefathers of the Belaanians were off-world transplant miners. Their descendants now lived in underground mazes of tunnels and catacombs, with almost no contact with other worlds—until Mapooly launched his People's Army. I had casually met a number of Belaanians on that visit, but none on a level of personal detail like what I was hearing now.

"After landing, Mapooly's guards took me deep into the planet's interior," Dhavail said. "I was brought before Beacheau. She was beautifully dressed in a soft cream gown, her deep brown hair adorned with pink and lavender petals. She was lying in a bed of white gold and crystal gems, unconscious. And Mapooly ordered me to pray."

If the situation wasn't so serious, if it wasn't the blood-thirsty General Mapooly that I had witnessed on Pharry, it would almost seem funny in an ironic way—a High Priest being ordered at blade-point to pray.

"I knew it was futile." Dhavail put his cup down. "Mapooly refused to accept that the Almighty Euranus did not violate the laws of the natural universe that He set in motion in the first place." Dhavail sighed. "But it was equally futile to refuse Mapooly's order, so I complied."

Of course he did. I caught myself with a sarcastic thought as I listened to the High Priest.

"We bowed our heads and prayed into the night. Hours passed. Evening and morning brought a new day. The next night, Beacheau grew flush and feverish, gasping for air. Mapooly knelt at her side and held her hand. I felt the depth of his anguish. But in my heart, I knew this was the way of life. The glistening gates of passage were opening before Beacheau. In an instant, she departed, and when she did, Mapooly reared his head and howled. I will never forget the words he uttered."

He squeezed his hands into tight fists. His eyes narrowed under slanted brows. His lips curled downward. For a split-second, I saw in Dhavail's face the savage beast within Mapooly that I witnessed on Pharry. Dhavail's face trembled as he reenacted Mapooly's words.

"'*Dox,* silent god of the universe, what sadism possesses you to sentence an innocent woman to a life of suffering and pain? What twisted conscience could crush the brevity of her happiness? To pass in silence is inexcusable. To withhold aid, unforgivable. What creator would exhibit such nefarious traits...but a nonexistent one?'"

I listened in silence, shocked at the spewing of hatred and cursing that I heard.

"'Euranus is nonexistent...!'" Dhavail's arms clenched into the air. "'...and I am left alone in a cold, impersonal universe. Woe to those who cross my path! They shall be snuffed out of existence.'" Dhavail looked at me. "'As my Beacheau was snatched from my embrace, I shall take and toss with the will of the gods.' Those were his exact words."

My muscles tightened, my heart pounding. If what Dhavail said was true, then General Mapooly was a madman, let loose by the grief of his loss, and wielding the most powerful military force in Eurania. With a single utterance, he could command destruction without mercy, without conscience, unstoppable.

"Mapooly turned to me with the eyes of the vile. I had never felt such a cold, piercing blackness from someone's gaze. I had never feared for my life before—until that moment. I saw his *rypniblade* hanging from his waist, and I pleaded for my life." He stopped, his eyes watering. "In my weakness, I offered something...unspeakable."

A compromise. I took a deep breath and steeled myself. Here, before me, was what I had suspected all along, the underhanded machinations that allowed the Temple institution and the High Clergy to survive centuries of occupation. I was surprised that the Monseigneur would tell me so readily. He verged on an emotional breakdown, his hands and cheeks trembling. His eyes seemed to plead for me to let him keep his secret.

"What did you offer?"

The High Priest heaved a sigh to summon his strength. The wait became agonizing, in its own right.

"I told Mapooly...." Dhavail took another deep breath. "I told him about a little-known mythical story of the Euranian Ancestors raising the dead back to life." Unable to contain them, tears began to roll down Dhavail's cheeks. "I offered to find out how to do this for him. How to raise Beacheau back to life." He dropped his face into his hands and wept. "I was thrown into a cell, shackled, abandoned in utter darkness."

I wasn't sure how I felt about the High Priest now—pitiful or dismissive. This man spoke to uncounted billions across far-flung worlds, ever the pragmatist. I wondered if this unheard-of story might have been something Dhavail made up to save his own skin. Still, complete isolation was a terrible ordeal for a seasoned soldier, let alone a civilian. "Did you...?" I might have sounded a bit unsympathetic, but this information was critical.

Dhavail shook his head with vigor. "Of course not! To do so would be an abomination against Almighty Euranus and His creation. I stalled as long as I could, then I was brought back before Mapooly —and another who was with him."

Another what? Obviously, not the executioner. Another priest? That wouldn't make sense, either. Beacheau was dead; stepping down to a lower priest would not serve Mapooly's purpose. I took a quick sip. The warmth soothed me. "Who?"

"When I came before Mapooly...." Dhavail shut his eyes, his hands clutched tight. "He had changed." Dhavail stared at me. "His eyes were no longer human. The irises shone a deep scarlet, like blood, with silver pupils sparkling like the flame of a candle. I thought I was looking at blood-stained blade-tips—mesmerizing, brilliant, but deadly from a depth of existence I'd never seen before. Mapooly laughed a maniacal howl that echoed off the walls."

I tried to gauge the Monseigneur's expression as he told the story. Did he really see what he said he saw, or had he suffered from hallucinations after his period of isolation? "Could there have been some unusual lighting to cause this?"

Dhavail shook his head. "The other man said to me, 'He will be the fulfillment of our prophecy.' We made eye contact, and I felt a sharp, piercing stab from the pitch-black pupils of this man's eyes.

Under his bald-dome head, the bushy ends of his slanted eyebrows seemed like wings that focused to the point of his nose. Mapooly said that, since I was unable to fulfill my promise, this other man would." Dhavail gasped for air as he struggled to describe the moment. "He had no further use for me and was prepared to kill me. But the other man intervened. He said, 'The Priest of Oscanos can make an excellent sacrifice.' And a hideous smile crept into Mapooly's face. Within hours, they transported me to Minoss for safekeeping."

"Who was he?" I was on edge, waiting for more information on this mysterious man.

The Monseigneur was on the verge of hyperventilation. "Zin Xothol, the High Priest of Luzomi. When he said his name, a horrible feeling swept over me. Mapooly was much more than just a military man who had fought and defeated the Revolutionary Guard. I was heartbroken. We were not entering an era of renewal after centuries of struggle and bloodshed. There would be no springtime for Etolis. General Mapooly looked like —and felt like—a phantasm, a mask for a deeper, darker terror of the kind unseen since the ancient days, when accounts of fact and fancy blended together." He took a deep breath to steady himself. "We are at the dawn of the age of Luzomi, the foretold reign of evil."

It was a good thing my office walls were bare. This was too much story, and not enough reality. I needed facts from a calm, rational man, not a fanciful religious interpretation from a priest who had proven he would say anything to preserve his own life.

Dhavail broke out of his narrative with a stark, pointed gaze. "You don't believe me, do you? You claim to be a believer because you know the stories. But like so many others, you don't believe in the reality of those teachings, do you?"

Gods or monsters—I wasn't sure if Dhavail could separate either from the real world around us. I leaned back in my chair and pondered what to do next with this man.

"Recall the stories you were taught as a child," Dhavail told us, once we reunited with the fleet.

I had positioned myself, Trophet, Genosser, and Kearn in a semi-circle, facing the High Priest. How long I could put up with these religious tales in my quest to gain useful information about Mapooly, I wasn't sure. That was why I brought my closest advisers into the office. Maybe the four of us, together, could glean something of value.

"In the beginning, Almighty Euranus created the universe. With it, the primordial beings came into existence: Lord Oscanos, Mother Gheriah, the Three Guardians—Cru, Thema, and Cqoeis—the dreaded Wa'ohl'thu, the heinous Luzomi, and their many assistants, the lower beings. To each, Euranus gave the power to create descendants, and each did, creating vast numbers of beings to follow in their footsteps." Dhavail lowered his voice. "The Euranian ancestors and descendants have been depicted through the millennia as grotesque beings, semi-humanoid and semi-bestial." He paused for a moment, looking each of us in the eye. "But we believe they are powerful entities composed of the very fabric of the universe, able to transition between matter and energy states as easily as we move between sleeping and waking states."

I raised an eyebrow. This was something unexpected—a departure from the familiar, strictly "spiritual" teachings. Could the High Priest be sharing privileged knowledge?

"Among the many creations of the Euranian Ancestors were our human forefathers and an earlier creation, Luzomi's reptiloid, the Troggle—a beast with limited intelligence, large orb-like eyes, small wings, and thumbs on its foreclaws. Mother Gheriah, aghast at the grotesque creature, banished it to a faraway, gaseous world. There, the bitter Luzomi secretly fashioned a mate with the aid of his two powerful lieutenants. One was the life-giving black avian, Jakkum, the subject of countless nightmarish works of art over the centuries. The other was the thundering, multi-podded, multi-eyed Neidemus. Together, they unleashed the cosmic forces of creation, drawing upon the very fabric of the universe to bring a she-mate to life. From this union, the Troggle spawned a legendary race of powerful warriors."

Genosser snuffed out his *cuira* stick and lit another. Trophet shifted in her seat. I could see Kearn stifle a yawn. I wasn't sure how this was related to Zin Xothol's appearance on Belaan, but I decided to hear the story out, on the chance that something important might come.

"The humans, however, possessed superior intelligence," Dhavail continued, "and with the ability to reproduce like no others, became too great a temptation to Luzomi. By subjugating the human race, Luzomi could possess an army greater than that of the terrible Troggle. Mother Gheriah turned to Oscanos to defend the humans from Luzomi's intentions, and a terrible cosmic war erupted between the forces of Luzomi and Oscanos.

"In the end, Oscanos threw down Luzomi and defeated him. The planets of Sigorum, where Luzomi reigned with his followers, and Amahl, where Oscanos and the others resided, were both rendered uninhabitable by the devastation. So Lord Oscanos relocated the humans, seeding them on the five founding planets—Memona, Jahop-thune, Paebih, Oscanos, and Hoscanis—where the human race flourished. And though he fled into exile with his followers, Luzomi's desire to rule over us never waned. To this day, he awaits the opportunity to effect his return."

This last part of Dhavail's narrative—the war—was familiar.

"Zin Xothol represents the latest in a long line of deviants who believe that Luzomi co-created the human race, and as such, is the rightful ruler of the human race." At last, the High Priest brought his tale back to the immediate developments. "They believe Luzomi's maleficent nature to be the true nature of humans. How many follow Xothol throughout Eurania, we don't know. Their identity stays in the shadows; they blend into everyday society. We don't even know who Zin Xothol is, in his normal guise." The High Priest's brows slanted. He eyed Genosser, then Kearn. "Nor do we know who around us is secretly a follower of Xothol and Luzomi."

I threw up my hands. "All right, Monseigneur, enough is enough." Religious doctrine was one thing, but casting unwarranted suspicion on my staff was uncalled for. "This other priest is interesting, but we need practical information about General Mapooly, something we can address as a fighting force. What can you offer along those lines?" Maybe I should have been gentler in my tone of voice, but these discourses were not what I had risked the lives of my men and women for. "Where are his forces being deployed, and for what purposes?"

Dhavail stopped and stared at me, as if affronted.

I could feel an outburst coming, but I had had enough of the scripture lesson. "Facts, Your

Holiness. We need hard facts."

The High Priest's lip trembled. "I know you have waged war to gain our freedom, using space fleets, laser cannons, and blades. But, you are blind—" He jabbed his finger at me like a drill boring into the depths of my existence. "*Blind* to the realm that our eyes cannot see. We face, not a military opponent, but a deity, perhaps our own creator."

I had to clear my head of all this, at least for a few minutes. Kearn and Trophet, hearing my call for a short break, bolted the office. No doubt, they had a list of status updates waiting for them. Genosser leaned back, started yet another new *cuira* stick, and closed his eyes.

I walked the main corridor of the ship, taking deep slow breaths to calm my tension, and paying no attention to the crew performing their duties. It was true that Monseigneur Dhavail was the beacon of the faithful in the dark age of chaos and confusion. Billions from hundreds of worlds trusted in his leadership with their lives. But I couldn't fathom his point of view. Worse, for all the work my men had put in, and the risk we took to rescue the High Priest, I had gained *nothing* in my understanding of Mapooly.

"Lord Walmsley?"

It was Rexold. I hadn't noticed how well she blended in with the three crewmen working on the environmental monitors. How long had she been watching me? The crewmen finished, packed their equipment, and departed. Rexold remained.

"Are you all right, sir?"

I gathered my thoughts before approaching her. "Your performance on the rescue was exemplary, Ms. Rexold."

"Thank you, sir." She bowed. "I hadn't expected the Monseigneur to be reluctant to being rescued."

In hindsight, it was understandable for the High Priest to have been too scared to risk an escape. My struggle now was the complete lack of reward for the risk. I was stumped, frustrated in my efforts to glean anything of use from the High Priest. My self-directed anger and my regret for undertaking this entire course of action was becoming a crushing weight, a blow to the gut that knocked the breath from my lungs.

I knew I needed a break from the High Priest, so I directed Rexold to a nearby window. Outside, the layered fabric of hyperspace whisked by. It would be a few more days before we returned to the central core regions of Eurania, where the main body of our fleet remained on patrol.

"Have you thought about where you'll be going, after the war is concluded?"

She shook her head. "I don't want to go home. There are only painful memories there. It hasn't been easy fitting in here, either. I'm not a soldier. But I believe in our calling to serve God, the Crown, and the innocent, and I've been happy that my work for the Corps has served a higher purpose. Maybe I'll enter a monastery and devote my life to my faith. It would be different, but in some ways, not really."

Her comments hit home. She wasn't a soldier, and I was, but neither of us had a place we could call "home." Although I was born on Alscras, I had spent my entire adult life in space, traveling from one war zone to another. The Corps was my home. Without my militia, what would I do with my life? Without a war to fight, I was directionless, leading the Corps through endless wanderings in space, on watch. For what?

Was I chasing a phantom? Why was I doggedly obsessing over General Mapooly? Because I didn't like the way he looked as Ostarand died? Or because I was scrambling for a reason to hold the Greyban Corps together?

Deep down, I still knew what I was feeling. Mapooly was dangerous. I couldn't prove it, but I had learned, over many years of life-and-death crises on the battlefields of Eurania, to trust my instincts. More to the point, I knew in my bones that High Priest Dhavail—the only person to stand face to face with Mapooly and resurface, free—held the key to confronting Mapooly with a reasonable chance of success. I had to re-direct his attention away from his entrenched teachings and back onto our immediate objective. General Mapooly.

Rexold was a woman of faith, one of the many

followers of the High Priest in the Greyban Corps. Could she help me reach him?

"The eyes," I said, after we reconvened around my desk, this time with Rexold between myself and Trophet. "What could have changed in General Mapooly? Did he become a follower of Zin Xothol?"

Monseigneur Dhavail sighed. "Mapooly is not just a follower, but a vessel of Luzomi."

"What do you mean?"

"Our eyes are the portals to that which is within us." Dhavail held his hands to either side of his face. "Within General Mapooly lies a spirit, bright as blood, shiny as silver, alive and active. He is now but a shell. Xothol must have invoked Luzomi, and now it inhabits Mapooly."

This was tiring. The suggestion seemed impossible. Did Xothol's appearance necessarily indicate the doings of demons and monsters in our midst? "Monseigneur," I offered a diplomatic tone of voice, "no disrespect intended, but we must consider the possibility of some more-realistic, scientifically based explanations." I looked to Trophet. "Don't we?"

Trophet nodded. "We do."

Dhavail folded his hands. "This is my interpretation of what I saw. I don't know how, but Luzomi has taken Mapooly, perhaps as his human lieutenant. You told me you were a believer, Lord

Walmsley. Are you a true believer of all things seen and unseen?"

I knew my definition of a "believer" did not include contemporary manifestations of the tales of long ago. I could feel the palms of my hands sweat. This line of discussion was more than uncomfortable for me.

Before I could get a word out, Dhavail gestured a brush off with his hand. "If your intention is to attack Mapooly, then I will tell you that you will be destroyed in the attempt." The High Priest's eyes and mine met in a solemn—contentious?—moment of silence. "Of course, it is for you to decide what course the many who follow you should undertake against this menace. But...." He pounded the desk. "You must believe!"

At least he conceded that it was my decision, but this was going nowhere.

"Perhaps...." Trophet tried to break the awkward silence, but even she could not get past her first word without faltering.

Rexold raised her hand, drawing a head turn from Genosser and a raised eyebrow from Kearn. Rexold quickly lowered her hand, clearly hesitant to interrupt Trophet.

"Okay, Ms. Rexold." I nodded my head toward her. I was determined to make progress of any kind. Might I get a breakthrough if I gave her a minute? "If what Monseigneur Dhavail says is true, then what do you think we can we do against him?"

Rexold bowed her head toward the High Priest and spoke quietly. "Monseigneur, can Luzomi be destroyed?"

Dhavail shook his head. "It is not for us to destroy Luzomi. That belongs to the realm of Almighty Euranus. He who created Luzomi can destroy Luzomi. We must be patient."

I didn't want to be patient. I wanted to jolt the Monseigneur into action. But that would, no doubt, be a terrible sin. I heard Kearn stifle a snicker. Then, Rexold raised her hand a second time, drawing puzzled looks from Genosser and Kearn. After I acknowledged her, Rexold bowed her head a second time.

"Monseigneur, Luzomi can't be destroyed, but he was defeated in the past. How? Is there a way that is still available to us?"

I nodded with approval. Rexold had brought up a possibility that none of us had considered. At least, it was a better starting point for tangible discussion than nothing.

Dhavail looked at the five of us, and I saw something in his eye. I could not describe why I felt this way, but it seemed like the High Priest knew of a way.

"Well?"

Rexold jolted in her seat. I didn't mean to raise my voice at the High Priest, but I was tired and wanted a straight answer.

Dhavail sighed. "In the distant past, the planet

Sigorum was destroyed with the *Partiixa*, a devastating weapon that Lord Oscanos created. And Luzomi himself was defeated with the aid of a weapon known as the *Gramm*."

So, there was hope. In his mind, at least. I could feel my heart start pounding. Finally, we had reached some useful information. I asked, "Where are these weapons now?"

Dhavail shook his head, his face downcast. "Nobody knows if the *Partiixa* still exists. The last recorded mention of it was discovered over one hundred years ago, on a tablet inscribed in what we now know to be the Apelian script."

"What about the *Gramm*?" I pressed.

Dhavail paused. "The *Gramm* magnifies and projects the will of its possessor. If handled properly, it is capable of shocking Luzomi back into the unknown recesses between the multiverses. The problem is that most people are far too disconcerted to achieve the transcendental focus required to power it."

He hadn't answered my question. "Does it still exist?"

Dhavail swallowed, hard. "Yes."

"Then it's our only hope, if we are to confront Mapooly." I was improvising like never before, rolling the dice on a course of action that I had no understanding about. I could only pray that it would be a worthwhile ploy. "We need to know where it is."

Dhavail looked at each of us again, silent. He pointed at me before answering. "I caution you—it is a weapon beyond a normal human's abilities, wielded by Lord Oscanos himself." He lowered his eyes.

"Well?"

Rexold's lip trembled. She was clearly disturbed by my repeated yelling at the High Priest. "Lord Walmsley, I beg you—"

Dhavail held up his hand. "It is all right, Ms. Rexold." Turning to me, the High Priest said with a grim voice, "It is in the deepest of the catacombs, far below the Temple at Mt. Weine, on Kelova."

I might have suspected. For what it was worth, we now had a concrete destination that coincided with Mapooly's ruthlessness. "Monseigneur," I said, sounding far more sure than I felt, "I do intend to seek out and attack General Mapooly. As powerful as he has become, and as grief-stricken as you describe him to be, he has become as dangerous a man as anybody Eurania has seen in the last six hundred years." I glanced at Kearn and Genosser; neither looked particularly enthusiastic. Trophet fidgeted. Rexold trembled. "Kelova has no strategic value, so I expect no military presence guarding it. Gentlemen, you will assess the damage Mapooly inflicted, while we recover the *Gramm*. Then we will move before Mapooly can launch a new attack."

3. *The Weapon of the Gods*

Among the ruins of Kelova, the Temple of Weine still stood, defiled with the devastation inflicted on the holy site by the fighting. Blackened craters pockmarked the grounds, blast holes permeated the walls, shattered glass littered everything, and black smoke poured out of a gaping maw ripped through the tower roof. Bodies littered the foyer floor, victims of the Belaanian slaughter.

As the troops fanned out to assess the damage, I watched High Priest Dhavail, tears streaming down his face, kneel beside each dead body and perform abbreviated last rites. We didn't have much time, but it was proper to give final blessings to the fallen innocent.

Nearby, Rexold stared at the devastation, silent. She began pacing about, and I wondered if she was wrestling with her own demons—the memories of the destruction of her home and family.

When he finished, Dhavail bowed his head and whispered a barely audible prayer. Then, without warning, he raised his hands into the air and cried out, "Almighty Euranus, your house is ransacked, your children slaughtered like animals. The beasts are like *wovren* in the night, demons from the fiery depths. When will you avenge this sacrilege? You must receive retribution!" His voice cracked. His energy spent, he collapsed in a heap, his head buried in his hands, sobbing.

Whatever I thought about his point of view, I could feel his torment. The slaughter of so many innocent victims was a pain as terrible as anything I had ever experienced in the battle. Mapooly was a monster who had to be stopped, without question.

Together with Rexold, I helped lift the High Priest to his feet as gently as I could.

"Come," Rexold said to Dhavail. "We must retrieve the *Gramm*."

Dhavail took several deep breaths, wiped his tears away, and with great effort, stifled his sobs and regathered his composure.

He led us down to the underground levels, below the archives, below even the vaults where physical records from the ancient days were kept, to the extensive subterranean burial grounds, where the remains of the great priests of the past lay in darkened silence. Three upper levels housed a collection of mausoleums, lined from wall to wall, and gallery to gallery, with elaborate tombs. In the lowest level, which was barely high enough to stand upright in, ancient sarcophagi lay on the original earthen ground that predated the construction of the temple.

Dhavail stopped at an unmarked tomb and shone his light on the plain stone block that covered the grave. Dropping to his hands and knees, he wiped away a thick layer of dust from the surface until he exposed a crease that marked a small compartment. He pried the door open, reached inside, and withdrew a small canvas bag. He untied the ropes that bound the bag and brought forth a dust-covered metal object—a vertical shaft tipped on both ends by bud-shaped finials, and crossed on both the top and bottom by similarly tipped horizontal bars.

"According to Scripture, Lord Oscanos overpowered Luzomi by channeling his will through the divine *Gramm*, until Luzomi was forced to flee," Dhavail said. "Later, the surviving humans were replanted, first to the planetoid Nathelia, then to Memona and the other founding worlds. To protect the humans from Luzomi, he passed the *Gramm* to Adelph, the only person whose connection to Oscanos was strong enough to power the *Gramm*. From the great Adelph, the *Gramm* passed to descending generations."

He glanced around the underground tombs, perhaps suggesting that some of those who had wielded the *Gramm* in the past may be lying around us.

"Nobody knows when, or under what circumstances, the *Gramm* appeared on Kelova. Some say it appeared to an Etolian High Priest in a vision. Others claim it was stolen during the dark ages by a clandestine cleric. Perhaps one of the many who lie in rest around us brought it with him. Regardless, it has been kept here, unknown to almost all, for the day when it is needed, again."

He held it out to me, the *Gramm* illuminated by his hand-light. Under dust and dirt, it looked dull, tarnished, and unremarkable, like a simple everyday metalwork. The top and bottom finials had noticeable circular depressions, as if they might have once held stones, perhaps decorative gems. I could not believe this was anything special, let alone a divine weapon. I glanced at Rexold. Did she believe the High Priest? Did Monseigneur Dhavail himself really believe what he was saying? I took a deep breath to boost my determination.

"Who is capable of powering it?" I asked.

Dhavail stared at me, his hands exhibiting a slight tremble. After taking three deep breaths, he said, "I will have to try."

The hesitation in Dhavail's voice wasn't inspiring.

As we traversed the Opa cluster, I contacted Admiral Nogine, commander of the Sestian armada and apprised her of our discussions with the High Priest. With two battleships rejoining Nogine's fleet after completing extensive repairs, the Sestian fleet now amounted to the second most powerful attack force, after Mapooly's, and was our best chance at confronting the People's Army, head to head. By engaging the Belaanian fleet, Nogine would give us a better opportunity to land and set up for our attack. After being pulled into battle against the Sestians, Mapooly would be forced to respond to our appearance on his home planet of Belaan.

I had many issues to contend with, foremost being Dhavail's role and his safety during the operation. We were heavily armed, and Dhavail had painted a picture of minimal security on guard during his captivity, but it still was a tremendous gamble. As we approached Belaan, the report arrived that the fleet battle had commenced. I dared not speculate on the losses Nogine would suffer.

Belaan was small and cold, a lone planet orbiting the star, D19028, which was the only luminous body occupying the void in the center of the Opa cluster. I remembered, from my first visit during my teen years, that the dark blue and gray cloud bands that layered over the planet surface rotated with a ferocity that wasn't apparent from space. On that occasion, I accompanied my father into the southern hemisphere mines. This time, we targeted General Mapooly's lair—the subterranean capital below the island of Gorroi.

Monseigneur Dhavail sat next to me in one of the landers. He proved unable to run very far with the full weight of our standard armor, so he dressed in lighter gear than the troops, with the *Gramm* tucked inside his hip pouch. His fists, resting on his lap, were clutched tight. His eyes were wide and barely blinking. I reached over and tapped his shoulder. In response, Dhavail glanced at me and took a deep breath to relax.

Realistically, I wasn't counting on the *Gramm* having any actual supernatural powers. We were bringing twelve dozen soldiers, a large mission squad for the Greyban Corps. We had one target— General Mapooly, dead or alive.

The counter below the front window began blinking amber. From my seat behind the pilot, I could see out the front window. The hangar doors of our carrier were parting, revealing angry, swirling clouds directly ahead. I didn't remember the atmosphere to be so torrential, but it was possible that, given my youth, my memory was faulty.

The blinker switched to solid red with a soft buzz.

"Here we go," the pilot said.

Half a dozen landers launched from our troop carrier. Our craft took the lead in the formation and entered the exosphere, the other landers flying alongside.

"Now entering the cloud cover," the pilot said.

The lander jolted. Dhavail tensed and hurriedly grasped the pouch holding the *Gramm*. Bolts of lightning exploded about us as we descended through miles of poisonous clouds, passing from one layer of whirling gas to another.

With the turbulence rocking the lander all the way down, Dhavail started to turn pale. I motioned to him to take slow, deep breaths. If he passed out, I would have no choice but to leave him in the lander while we disembarked.

"There it is," the pilot said.

The clouds parted before us to reveal Gorroi. It was a large island lined by high cliffs, rocky and barren except for a small collection of stone buildings in the interior valley. There were no signs of life in the compound—no lights, no movement. The comm unit picked up no broadcast signals. It was hard to believe that this could be the origination point of the massive People's Army.

"Over there." I pointed out a nearby formation of tall rocks that could camouflage our arrival. "All troops, prepare to disembark."

I glanced at Dhavail. He looked okay. As the men lined up at the door with their life-support helmets on and their rifles readied, the Monseigneur rose from his seat to join them.

After landing, Genosser and I led our men on foot toward the compound. We jumped the few duty guards that we encountered at close quarters, taking them out with blades only. We then entered an airlock. After disposing of the lone sentry standing watch at the entrance to the underground complex, I lifted my helmet visor for a quick look around, then motioned for the Monseigneur. High Priest Dhavail stepped forward and guided us down into the planet's interior core.

Level by level, we traversed what looked like utility corridors, a few of which were wide enough for three people at a time. Many were so cramped that the men had to crouch in single file. Most were dimly lit by small lights spaced far apart along one wall. Twice, we entered a pitch black tunnel. I couldn't help but wonder about the path we were following. Perhaps Mapooly had taken Dhavail this way so that the Monseigneur wouldn't see too much. I was impressed that Dhavail remembered the way with as much certainty as he was exhibiting.

Reaching the end of a particularly long corridor, Dhavail stopped in front of a closed door and waved to Genosser. No doubt, we were nearing the place where he had been taken before. Genosser stepped forward with a dozen men and after I nodded, Dhavail opened the door, revealing the brightly lit interior of a rock cavern. Metal doors and dimly lit tunnel entrances surrounded us. A pair of utility workers in drab brown overalls and gray helmets walked by. Genosser's men charged out, forced the workers down to the ground, and ran toward each of the tunnel entrances with their rifles pointed.

A nearby group of about a dozen Belaanians workers shouted and stared to run away. Genosser threw a switch on his rifle and fired a smoke burst that enveloped the Belaanians, bringing them to their knees, choking. A second group of five or six Belaanians screamed and ran for a second tunnel. They were smothered by a second soldier's smoke bomb. A third group threw up their hands and fell to their knees. Like lightning, our soldiers surrounded everybody, their rifles pointed at the cowering workers, while more soldiers took up positions guarding the far ends of the corridors.

Dhavail pointed toward a set of bronze double doors on the far side of the cavern. Genosser and I ran after him with a dozen men. Surprisingly, he went past the double doors and cracked open a small side door. We followed him in and found ourselves in a short, unlit access tunnel. Before us was a magnificent chamber with circular walls and a crystal domed ceiling, twenty-five feet high. To our left, charcoal gray smoke poured out of a cauldron. To our right, five seven-foot-tall marble statues of two- and four-footed beasts lined the wall.

In the center of the otherwise unoccupied chamber, we discovered the black-robed, bald-headed Zin Xothol performing a ritual on Beacheau, who was lying in a bed of white gold and crystal.

"Hicithe, cislemae, jaka-jakae...." He chanted in what sounded to me like ancient Etolian.

With one hand on her head, and the other on her waist, he sang a soft, atonal melody. A strange golden light emitted from his two hands as he mumbled the words.

"Y'jili anhannou pakoso,
"Lhuzomi, ghethi bayillou Euranua,
"ghethi bayilou universalia,
"Euranua, gomourouh."

He levitated off the ground an inch, then returned back to the floor. Again, he rose, this time two inches, before settling down again. He rested his head on her chest, and his feet rose again, this time remaining an inch off the ground. As he floated, a soft golden glow developed around his head—a comforting glow that clashed with the words Xothol chanted.

"Lhuzomi gartha,
"Lhuzomi pixui,
"Lhuzomi antizio,
"Lhuzomi hellui."

The repetitive invocation of Luzomi's name seemed something of the dark magic cited in the ancient Etolian myths, something very primitive, unnatural, and unholy. I looked to Dhavail, who was now mouthing a prayer with his eyes closed, the *Gramm* held tight in his fist.

"Lhuzomi ea," Xothol continued, *"Lhuzomi ku, Lhuzomi xi...."*

As Xothol settled down to the floor, his glow faded. A side door opened.

Mapooly walked in.

Apparently, he had sent his fleet into combat while he stayed with his dead wife. His eyes were normal—not as Dhavail had described—and it was touching to see Mapooly take her hands. Conflicting thoughts rushed into my mind about the Monseigneur's stories: Beacheau's death, Mapooly's eyes. Could the High Priest have been mistaken? Did Dhavail get his facts all jumbled up? The smile on Mapooly's face felt different than what he had showed at Ostarand's execution. It seemed gentle, almost tender, with a genuine humanity. Could I be wrong about Mapooly's intentions?

But then, Beacheau's eyes opened. As Mapooly helped her up, Dhavail uttered a gasp at the sight of Beacheau's bright red and silver sparkling eyes. Mapooly smiled at her, and she smiled back.

"e'Thuq?" she asked. Did her slight voice stir an echo in the chamber?

In contrast to Mapooly's, Beacheau's smile felt cold, mechanical, without the natural buoyancy that came with human joy. She did not feel alive as Mapooly did.

"Behold," Xothol presented Beacheau to Mapooly, "Lord Luzomi has returned your love to you."

"Beacheau...." Mapooly whispered, lifting his hand to his wife's cheek.

This was our chance. With Mapooly and Xothol both occupied by Beacheau's rising, I was about to signal our riflemen. Suddenly, Dhavail yanked me aside with a hard pull. To my horror, the High Priest of Kelova stormed past me, out of the shadows of the hallway where we stood, revealing our position to Mapooly and placing all of us in imminent danger. Stonefaced, Dhavail held the *Gramm* up, the metalwork now exhibiting a strange green shine.

"By the power of Oscanos," Dhavail called out, "I cast you out!"

Beacheau's face contorted as she howled like a wild bird.

"No!" Xothol yelled.

Dhavail wrapped both hands about the *Gramm* and a greenish beam of light projected out from it, enveloping Beacheau in a green halo. She screamed, and as she struggled from inside the halo, a silhouette-like figure appeared within her now-translucent body. It had a small head, large orbs, a gaping mouth, and a mass of tentacles that writhed about, pushing outward against her body. A low moan sounded. I had never seen anything like it before in my life.

"Beacheau!" Mapooly cried, thrown back from her grasp by the powerful halo.

The silhouette figure burst into a splattering of tiny, splotch-like shadows. The greenish beam faded, the black splotches dissipated from sight, and when the halo disappeared, Beacheau collapsed back onto the bed, lifeless. Xothol and Mapooly both rushed to her side. I ran in, past the gaping Dhavail, my men following with their weapons drawn.

"General Mapooly!" I yelled. "Freeze!"

Mapooly whirled on me, his eyes now radiating a shiny red and silver eeriness.

I froze at the sight—and with a speed I'd never seen before, he drew his *rypniblade* and rushed at Dhavail. I leaped as far as I could, yanking out my *rypniblade*, and managed to deflect Mapooly's swipe so that he missed Dhavail's head by inches. As the High Priest scrambled away, Mapooly wailed a *drakothon*'s cry.

"Stop or I'll shoot!" Genosser pointed his rifle at Mapooly.

Mapooly snarled and whirled on Genosser. Genosser fired, the exploding energy bolt stunning Mapooly for but a moment.

It was impossible. The shot should have killed Mapooly in a bloody explosion, but it hardly delayed him.

Not even scratched, Mapooly cut his long-blade across Genosser's rifle, hacking off the front of the barrel and forcing Genosser to flee. With my free arm, I jerked my charge-pak rifle into position. I gave the order to open fire and unleashed my rifle's deadly blast.

Mapooly, struggling against a barrage of explosions that failed to draw even a single drop of blood, slammed backward against the bed, pinned by the cascade of energy pounding him. With his arms and legs flailing like marionette limbs, Mapooly lost his balance and fell to the ground beside the bed.

But then, out of the corner of my eye, I saw Zin Xothol rip a chain off his neck and raise a medallion into the air, crying out,

"Lhuzomi, aa-thok-qui,

"Kou, kou, kou, ea kont tu—"

I pivoted and fired, blasting Xothol into a bloody heap, dead. The medallion shattered into uncounted splinters against the wall. But it was too late. A split-second whirling stream of energy from the medallion had projected up into the crystal ceiling, causing a swirling light to appear. It rotated as a pinwheel, emitting a sickly greenish light with puffs of pink and gray exploding throughout. The light expanded as it revolved until it was wide enough to stretch over the entire dome. A shadow appeared in the center of the light sphere, a pitch black, multi-limbed being that writhed and fluctuated in size and shape as it emerged from the swirling light.

The whirling rays stretched to bathe Mapooly in a blinding, prism-like halo that expanded to monstrous proportions. Another silhouette figure materialized and enveloped Mapooly. The shadow had a pointy beak, an oversized horned head, large talons, humanoid forearms, and wings that were prevented from extending by the halo's field. A monstrous roar echoed throughout the chamber.

"It is Jakkum!" Dhavail cried.

It stretched ten to twelve feet in length from head to toe, with a long serpentine tail that ended in four- to five-foot-long spikes. I was stunned, not sure whether the creature that was starting to resemble Luzomi's black avian lieutenant was still Mapooly or not. As it fought to right itself, it drew bright sparks from the interior of the halo wherever it touched it. The brilliant flashes of energy seemed to dilute the halo's power field, and the greenish color faded. Without warning, the halo disappeared, and the silhouette settled into physical form.

A rough scaly skin covered Mapooly's face, and a crust of feather-shaped flakes grew to cover the scales. Large pointed horns topped his head; his beak, with a slender tongue flickering in and out, filled with sharp fangs. His eyes, the pupils completely gone, turned into blood red orbs. The sight terrified me as to both what he had become, and what was within him.

The Mapooly creature whipped to its side and, before I could react, wrapped its tail around Dhavail and yanked him down to the ground in mid-cry. Its foreclaw reached across and ripped the *Gramm* out of Dhavail's grasp, flinging it into the corner. I couldn't fire at the beast without killing Dhavail, so I dropped my rifle and summoned all my strength to hack at the creature's head with my *rypniblade*. The blade sunk several inches into the flesh of its face and stuck like industrial adhesive. It flung its head to one side, yanking the stuck *rypniblade* from my grasp. I lost my balance and fell hard to my hands and knees. Its wings then extended and it rose into the air, like the many famous depictions of Jakkum painted through the centuries.

I could only stare at the sight of the creature ascending toward the swirling light—and the black, multi-limbed being within—with the flailing Dhavail still captive in its tail's grasp. At that moment, in a crisis of life and death unlike anything I had ever experienced in my two decades on the battlefield, the sight of the inert *rypniblade* protruding from the creature's head finally made me understand.

High Priest Dhavail had been right. I was kneeling not before a mythical story, but the real Luzomi and his lieutenant.

Blades were useless. Our most advanced charge-pak rifles were equally useless. I had no doubt that even ship-mounted space-cannons would be just as useless. I dashed the short distance to where the *Gramm* lay and took it in my hands. The weapon of Lord Oscanos was our only hope for survival.

"Die, demon—argh!" Dhavail cried with determination.

I pointed my arms toward the center of the Jakkum's chest and aimed the *Gramm*...

...and a bottomless, cold blackness enveloped me. All sense of direction disappeared. I fell headfirst through a foul rot, a stench that trailed through a starless void.

The Great Nebula at the center of the Euranian

star cluster appeared in the distance and accelerated toward me with blinding speed. I penetrated the outermost layers of plasma gas and whooshed toward two metallic-gray worlds orbiting a giant red star. Purely on instinct, I tried to pull away from the larger planet, which was engulfed in an overpowering malodor, a mixture of a decaying rot and sulphur. The smaller globe was blanketed by a thick, purple haze at twilight. Descending beneath the cloud cover, I began to sense the presence of the Euranian Ancestors: Lord Oscanos, Mother Gheriah, and the Three Guardians, Cru, Thema, and Cqoeis, though I could not see anything but haze.

And from the midst of their presence, a brilliant light burst forth, rippling waves of rainbow-like energy that flowed over and through my fingers, warm, alive...

...and I cast two hot-white beams of energy from the top and bottom finials of the *Gramm* onto Mapooly's heart.

The explosion of blood knocked us all backward to the ground. The concussion cracked the far wall and the full length of the ceiling. Alarms blared. Blue and white emergency lights flashed. The ear-piercing cry of the *drakothon* reverberated through the chamber. We were all doused with a downpour of blood and smothered by the stench of *pomira* bark blown about by the flapping of invisible wings. A slimy tentacle brushed my waist and tiny claws lightly scratched my shoulder.

I turned, unsure of what I would find behind me, but saw no visible creature around me—or anywhere in the chamber.

"Catch him!"

Genosser and several soldiers ran into position to catch the falling, screaming Dhavail. With his arms and legs flailing, the High Priest hit the men at an awkward angle. As the entire group crumpled to the ground, Dhavail cried out in pain as he reached for his right leg.

Nearby, the Mapooly creature smashed hard to the ground, floor tiles ricocheting into the air, the *rypniblade* rebounding away with a clang, a cloud of red vapor spraying upward from the body like a fountain.

I was hyperventilating, my nerves raw and shaking, my hands still clutching the blood-stained *Gramm*. Hearing Dhavail's cry, I ran to him and the pile of men in the center of the chamber. "Are you hurt?" The wind died as I reached them. The overhead pinwheel light faded and the howl echoed away. Dhavail's hysterical cries resonated about us.

Two of the soldiers rolled over and attended to Dhavail. One raised his hand into the air. "We need a splint!"

I grasped Dhavail's shoulder. Catching a split-second glance at his leg, I could tell that his knee was fractured. "We'll take care of you."

More men ran over, two pulling medi-kits out of

their hip pouches. As they worked on the High Priest, Genosser rose to his hands and knees and looked up. Overhead, I saw vapors leaking in through the cracked dome.

"The barrier's been compromised," one of the soldiers said, reading his digi-com. "The atmosphere's going."

"We'd better hurry," Genosser told the medics.

"Done." One medic fastened the splint while a second injected Dhavail with a painkiller.

"Come on," I urged. Out of the corner of my eye, I saw my charge-pak rifle and my *rypniblade*, both lying useless on the ground. I wedged the *Gramm* under my belt and got to my feet, pausing to steady my legs. The dead bodies of Beacheau, Xothol, and the bloody, chest-gouged Mapooly, somehow reverted back to human form, lay nearby. "This planet's better off buried with its dead."

Genosser and I helped Dhavail up and onto the back of one of soldiers. With the troops leading the way behind a steady wall of weapons fire, the High Priest rode piggyback and we retreated through the maze of tunnels.

We exited the compound and released the emergency airlock, sealing the interior behind us. I looked back and saw through a small window some of the pursuing soldiers, locked inside, scrambling about and falling from the poisonous gases that rushed in. We soon reached our ships and launched into space, leaving behind the nightmare world of

Belaan and the memories of Mapooly.

On the deathly silent ride back out of the Opa Cluster, I sat with Dhavail. While the soldiers about us attended to their injuries, Dhavail's painkiller took effect and he fell asleep. Reflecting on the experience we had just survived, I couldn't help but ponder the Monseigneur, and how wrong I had been about him.

As for the People's Army, news of Admiral Nogine's showdown with Mapooly's fleet spread like wildfire throughout Eurania. Leaderless, the Belaanians still fought to the bitter end and both fleets were devastated. Admiral Nogine herself managed to survive a suicide ramming of her flagship. Only a small handful of Belaanian ships escaped; the rest perished.

When he recovered from the injuries he sustained from the fall, High Priest Dhavail informed me of his decision to redact all accounts of the destruction of Belaan to expunge any references to the horror of Luzomi's incursion. I knew this was necessary to prevent the general chaos and social breakdown that would erupt from such a revelation.

So, with the main body of the Belaanian fleet destroyed, with General Mapooly and Zin Xothol both dead, and with Luzomi seemingly turned away by the power of the *Gramm*, all fighting soon died away.

Epilogue

Finished with his tale, Metiar Walmsley excused his audience of ten clerical novices. At the sound of approaching footsteps, he turned his head. A middle-aged man of short stature and plain tan business dress approached with two muscular men in sleeveless white tunics in tow.

"Lord Walmsley," Dubian Trophet said, "Monseigneur Dhavail is asking for you." Walmsley's Chief of Staff kneeled and lowered his voice. "He is weakening." Trophet's eyes cast downward. "I fear he may be near his time."

Walmsley sighed with a heavy heart. He sat in his high-backed, thick-cushioned chair on the portico, covered from his shoulders to his feet by a heavy, patch-patterned quilt. Removing his wire-rimmed spectacles, he closed his tired eyes and soaked in the warmth of the gentle breeze. After taking in a deep breath, he opened his eyes and looked at the pink sunset illuminating the sky. He then returned his lightweight glasses to his deep-wrinkled face. Below his overlook, the lights of the town of Frenius were turning on.

Even after four decades of living on this idyllic world of Wichloc, he still hadn't tired of the view of the magnificent tropical forests that lay beyond the borders of the settlements. But the loneliness never ceased. Trophet motioned for the two muscle men to stand ready to assist while Walmsley grasped the hilt-shaped handle of his bronze-colored cane and rose to his feet.

As they made the slow walk through the stone corridors of the ancient fortress, Walmsley remembered the many joys he and High Priest Dhavail had shared since arriving on this planet. The many outings they led into the forests to view the wildlife. The many town gatherings they presided over to celebrate a wedding, a new home, or a birth. So much happiness over such an extended period of time.

Walmsley and his men reached the eastern residence wing and came before a large arched wooden door decorated with a mosaic depicting the forests of ancient Amahl. Trophet nudged the door open and they entered. Inside, the men accompanied Walmsley through the front parlor, where half a dozen men and women—members of the town council—sat in silence. Proceeding past the townsfolk, they entered a low-lit, spacious bedroom in the back.

A second gathering of six men and women in heavy white robes—members of the clergy—rose from their knees at the foot of the oversized bed to greet Walmsley.

"Monseigneur Navilla," Walmsley addressed the leader of the clergymen. Even now, Walmsley needed to remind himself that the "young man" had long ago reached his prime, his hairline already receding, and that he would soon be the next Head Priest of their people. "How is your father?"

The downcast look in Navilla's eyes saddened Walmsley.

"He seems delirious, and his breathing is difficult," Navilla said, "but he is at peace." He stepped forward and placed his hand on Walmsley's arm. "My father would be happy to see you."

"Thank you." Walmsley offered Navilla a gentle smile before stepping to the bedside.

Whinn Rexold sat beside the ailing High Priest praying with one hand resting on Dhavail's arm, and the other grasping a string of wooden beads. Seeing Walmsley approach, Rexold released the High Priest's arm and rose to her feet.

Walmsley held up his hand and motioned for Rexold to sit back down. The gray-haired consort of the High Priest was not much younger than Dhavail and Walmsley. There was no need for her to vacate her seat. Navilla stepped up and positioned a chair for Walmsley to sit in.

As Rexold continued her quiet prayers, Walmsley gazed at his old friend, who was lying in silence under a soft, golden blanket, an occasional breath interrupting long moments of stillness. Dhavail's eyes were closed. Walmsley took Dhavail's hand and slid his purple and gold wristband—which the Monseigneur had blessed and given to him a couple decades ago—from his wrist to Dhavail's.

The old High Priest smiled and his eyes opened a slit. His mouth moved, but no words sounded.

"Just rest," Walmsley said, squeezing Dhavail's hand. "I will stay with you." He thought about their past.

How ironic that he had just recounted their first meeting to a new generation. The tale had brought the experience back with a powerful vividness—his views of the High Priest, first as a figurehead, then as someone steeped in untold secrets and mysteries, and finally as the one man who challenged the ancient Deity of Darkness.

The war had worn everyone out beyond exhaustion. With its conclusion, and the eventual formation of the new Euranian order, Walmsley withdrew the Greyban Corps to this remote world. Within a year of this retirement from service, Monseigneur Dhavail also stepped down from the priesthood, citing the need for fresh leadership not tainted by the decades of war. He quickly turned the Temple of Wiene, and the monumental task of reconstruction, over to a new High Priest and journeyed to Wichloc, joining Walmsley for a respite and recovery that flowered into a lifelong friendship.

As for the all-powerful *Gramm*, the entire experience still summoned feelings of sheer terror, even after the passing of half a lifetime. Walmsley kept it locked away in a vault known only to himself and Dhavail. But though it was out of sight, it was not out of mind. Neither was the memory of Luzomi.

For Walmsley, the new life on Wichloc became his long-sought opportunity to reflect upon a new outlook on life, and to take up a new and urgent purpose. He lay down his arms and, under Dhavail's tutelage, slowly and systematically studied what he had formerly dismissed as long-outdated mythical tales. *The Songs of the Euranians* contained the compendium of ancient stories of the Euranian Ancestors and the age-old annals of the early Euranian people. Perhaps the prophesied return of Luzomi would not occur in their lifetime, Dhavail had told him, but as the only other man able to invoke the power of the *Gramm*, Walmsley's mission now had to be the mastery of spiritual warfare. So they spent the passing decades preparing for a larger battle.

Dhavail turned his head toward Walmsley. His mouth formed a word. Walmsley bent down to listen.

"...home...."

Walmsley felt a hint of a squeeze in his hand. He couldn't help but smile. For all the many years and decades they had lived here, the old priest never forgot where he truly belonged. Once a spiritual leader, always a spiritual leader, and the spiritual beacon of the Euranian people was the Temple of Wiene on Kelova.

"All right, my friend," Walmsley said. "I'll take you home."

Walmsley felt a second, much more powerful, squeeze in his hand. The High Priest's body tensed. Navilla rushed forward to join Walmsley and Rexold as Dhavail gasped, his body stiffening.

Rexold took the High Priest's free hand, held it tight, and closed her eyes. A tear rolled down her cheek.

"Mother Gheriah," Navilla prayed, "smile upon my father's face. Lord Oscanos, lift him up."

Walmsley placed his free hand on Dhavail's soft cap and cradled his old friend's head. Dhavail released his breath and relaxed his body. His eyes closed. Walmsley also closed his eyes and lowered his head, the blanket of sadness engulfing him. He heard Rexold and Navilla weep.

Trophet said, "The High Priest, our dear Father, our friend and guide, has departed. Ring the bell, nine tolls, and let the people begin nine days of mourning."

Walmsley lifted his head and saw the other

members of the clergy kneel at the foot of Dhavail's bed, bow, and chant a short prayer. After they finished, they rose and covered High Priest Dhavail with his golden blanket.

"We will begin preparations for your ascension," one of the clergymen said to Navilla.

One of the clergywomen embraced Rexold. "We are all saddened."

They all bowed to her, then to Navilla, and finally to Trophet before departing in silence.

"Lord Walmsley," Trophet said, "what are your wishes?"

"I don't know." Walmsley slowly shook his head. "I would like some time."

"Understood, sir." Trophet bowed and left with the two muscle men. They closed the bedroom chamber doors as they departed.

Now alone, Walmsley gazed at Rexold and Navilla. Except for the tears in their eyes, both were stoic in dealing with their grief. "The High Priest's last wish was to be taken home." He paused to assess whether they understood his meaning. "I would like the two of you to accompany me on the journey."

"To where?" Navilla asked.

Walmsley paused. Like the other members of his generation, Navilla had been born here on Wichloc and had never traveled off planet. The core worlds of the Central Empire were only names of faraway locations.

It had been nearly half a century with no signs of trouble. Walmsley's eyes met Rexold's. It was now time to contemplate the inevitable return.

"To the Great Temple on Kelova." Walmsley saw Rexold nod her head. "There, the Monseigneur will rest with the other great priests of Euranian history. There, we will return the *Gramm* to its proper holding place, for the day when it will be called upon, again."

Rexold tensed for a moment. Walmsley knew that the memories of the tombs of the great priests remained fresh in her mind.

With the passing of Monseigneur Dhavail, Walmsley now had to consider the possibility that Luzomi's prophesied return would not occur until a future generation. He didn't know who would be the next wielder of the *Gramm*. Rexold had vehemently refused on numerous occasions to take it. Navilla had expressed similar reservations, citing the need to strengthen his inner faith before considering such an undertaking. Perhaps some mild-mannered member of Navilla's generation would eventually emerge. Regardless, it was important for somebody other than just Walmsley to know where to retrieve the *Gramm*. By bringing both Rexold and Navilla to Kelova, he would be reasonably assured that the knowledge of the *Gramm* would be passed on.

"I understand," Navilla quietly said.

Walmsley took a deep breath to clear his mind. "After the period of mourning has concluded, we will begin preparations. But for now, let us honor the memory of the High Priest." He put his hand on Rexold's shoulder. She looked at him through her tears. "He was a great man and a powerful spiritual leader. Someday, he will be revered for the historic victory he achieved."

Rexold managed a smile. "Thank you, Lord Walmsley."

Navilla bowed and accompanied Rexold out.

With the help of his cane, Lord Walmsley walked alone to the chapel. Entering through the double doors, he paused and looked about, remembering the countless services High Priest Dhavail had led through the decades. Foremost among these memories were the myriad of holy festivals, both the traditional holidays from the Kelovan Temple and new observances created by the Corps population. He walked up to the chair in the front row where he always sat, now an empty chair among many empty chairs. He settled in and gazed at the altar. The chapel was devoid. The chapel *felt* devoid.

He stared at one of the paintings on the wall. It was a portrait of Lord Oscanos, whose taut upper-body muscles and slanted eyebrows expressed the intensity of a life-and-death war. His enemy was a gray-brown scaly serpent, horned and winged, with a tail coiled tight around Oscanos' legs. Behind them, throngs of bloodied and battered humans and reptiloids fought.

A sudden rush of disquiet pressed down upon Walmsley, a cold vacuum of emptiness trailing off into the void of time and space. The feeling chilled Walmsley.

The last time he felt something like this was fifty years ago, when he and Monseigneur Dhavail were locked in a battle to the death against General Mapooly.

As a distant bell began tolling, Walmsley's thoughts returned to the old High Priest. Of all the people who had settled on Wichloc after the war, Dhavail and Rexold were the last surviving members of Walmsley's generation, besides Walmsley himself. Together, they had survived the otherworldly terror of General Mapooly. Now, in this garden world, far away from the new Central Empire and surrounded by the children and grandchildren of his late followers, Lord Walmsley felt alone, with only his memories, Dhavail's teachings, his new mission, a faint foul feeling that brushed by...and the most powerful weapon ever created at his disposal.

The End

The Galactic Revolutions

A Summary
by Moses Solomon

Six hundred years of Saolian occupation—the Dark Age of Eurania—and the memories of the golden era of the ancient Etolian empire had long since faded into a collection of tales. Myths. Legends.

The Galactic Revolutions was not a single rebellion. Even modern historians have not reached consensus on an agreed-upon opening salvo.

The war started small with guerilla raids in the Outer Territories. Notably absent from the list of outlying fighters were the miners of Belaan. Among the most distant of the Eurania worlds, the mysterious Belaanians remained quiet, silent, and invisible for over two decades while battles erupted all along the perimeter of the star cluster.

As the Saolians conscripted more and more central Euranians into their military ranks to battle the tribes from the Outer Territories, new rebellions broke out—this time on the core worlds of Sestia, Bexel, Breame, Kearo, and Alscras. With multiple brushfires to combat on multiple fronts, the Saolians could only signal their home—the faraway star cluster of Fembourne—and wait for additional help. But even if auxiliary units embarked on the long journey, the reinforcements would not be in time. A decade later, a new movement—the Revolutionary Guard of Pharry, led by Chairman Rai Ostarand—entered the war, slaughtering the backpedaling Saolians without mercy. After six hundred years of occupation, the weight of foreign domination was finally overthrown.

In its place was a mighty star horde, a new homegrown terror. The Revolutionary Guard swept across central Eurania, destroying one planet after another, eventually driving far out into the Outer Territories—until they reached Belaan, and the mysterious fighting force that would finally bring the Revolutions to its end.

A violent jolt rocked the spacecraft, interrupting Morgan and Rayna's climactic moment.

"*Dox!*" Morgan cursed as an alarm blared. Nothing could be more annoying than to be stopped by a blown engine relay. But, alone out here in space, anything more than that would be a real problem.

Another alarm sounded just as a mass of multi-colored particles streaked past the front window. Another tremor shook the little ship, forcing Rayna to brace herself against the back of her seat as she got up. Outside the window, the layered folds of hyperspace collapsed around them and a starfield settled into place.

Morgan's mind raced. What kind of particle beam could break out of normal space? Checking the monitor, he saw the blue-green world of Volon come into view, just as another beam—one that covered the entire width of the front window—fired from the planet. "Hang on, Rayna!" The strike sent rough shivers through the craft.

"Who's shooting at us?" Rayna asked as she checked the telemetry data from the shot.

This was one mystery Morgan wanted no part of. The Buggy broadcasted no military signals and to his knowledge, Volon wasn't advanced enough to build a weapon like this. He switched off the autopilot, took hold of the steering yoke, and fired the boosters to pull the craft away from Volon. "Get the life-suits."

Rayna reached up and released the overhead compartment, allowing two bright orange emergency jumpsuits to roll out. She tossed Morgan's bundle onto the helmet-hook next to him, and quickly donned her suit, fastening the quick-action seals, and hanging the helmet on the hook next to her side of the console.

"Can this Buggy take all this?" Rayna strapped herself into her seat and took the controls.

"Don't know." Morgan quickly zipped into his jumpsuit and strapped himself back into his seat. "*Tatiki!*" he cursed, struggling with the steering. "The handling stinks."

"I *told* you to take the Comet," Rayna scolded, "instead of this piece of—"

A wide, twisting band of light, streaming all the colors of the rainbow, lanced out from Volon and smothered the front and side windows, completely enveloping the Buggy. A hot-pink bolt of energy leaped out from a vent, arced across the instrument panel, and struck the bank of data monitors, shorting out two of the gauges in a shower of sparks. Morgan's hands jerked loose of the yoke as the bolt flashed through the steering column.

He pivoted his head at the sound of Rayna's scream. Struck by the bolt in a blinding flash of light, she lurched into convulsions...

About the author:

After a successful 25-year career in the utility industry, Moses Solomon set sail on a new career journey as a science fiction/fantasy writer. His first publication, ***The Santamobile***, a tale of Santa Claus in the 21st century, received the following words of praise:

"...even readers not into fantasy will enjoy this nice short Christmas story."

"What can I say? This is a really well put-together book that everyone preteen and up should read..."

Moses Solomon is also the author of two new science fiction novellas, both set in the Euranian star cluster. ***The Terror of Mapooly*** introduces the spacefaring Euranians at the end of the Galactic Revolutions.

The Euranian setting is revisited in ***Timegazer***, which takes place fifty years later.

Follow Moses Solomon's tales of Eurania at **http://eurania.wordpress.com/** and on Twitter (**@MoSolomon299**).

Also by Moses Solomon
The Santamobile
a tale of Santa in the 21st century

Scooter, diminutive among the other elves and far younger, squinted over the tops of the evergreen forest at the billowing, angry clouds rolling in from the southeastern sky. The faint whisper of a frosty breeze ruffled the highest of the overhead branches. The crowd of about a hundred fur-clad elves and uncounted forest animals that milled about the expansive clearing stayed quiet. It was almost midnight of the 25th, a full twenty-four hours since the team had departed for their annual sojourn around the world, following the time zones as the earth rotated below them.

There hadn't been a year like this one in a long time. Scooter thought back to his childhood, and the year of the Great Blizzard. That historic storm had been an anomaly. Scooter wasn't sure if this year's was or not. Like everyone else in the elf community, he kept abreast of the current news by picking up the available satellite broadcasts. According to most of the latest scientific publications, the earth was warming and changing, the atmosphere growing more temperamental and tempestuous. The worldwide weather forecast this Christmas Eve had been for violent pockets of turbulence and an abundance of storm systems throughout the northern hemisphere. Scooter couldn't help but dwell on how Santa would fare, under these conditions.

The roar of a motor interrupted his thoughts. A snowmobile emerged from behind a grove of evergreens, snow kicking up in its wake as it descended the knoll. Inside, the Chief of Staff, the imposing (for an elf) Piotr, and the chief mechanic and Scooter's team leader, Serge, accompanied a bundled-up Mrs. Claus.

Scooter smiled at the sight of Mrs. Claus. Right on time, as usual, her appearance signaled that their long wait was almost over.

Serge drove the snowmobile into the taxi area and brought it to a stop amidst the elves. Piotr helped Mrs. Claus, clutching her thick thermal muffler while still sipping her large tea mug, step out onto the snow. Questions immediately peppered her from all directions.

"What's the latest weather report, Mrs. Claus?"

"Should we prepare blankets?"

"Do you think Santa got airsick?"

Mrs. Claus released her muffler and raised her free hand. "I only know..." Her steady, clear voice calmed the murmur. "...that Santa always appreciates a refill for his cider mug, upon landing." She gave everyone a warm, gracious smile. "I'm sure he'll have plenty of stories for us about this year's trip."

Scooter smiled. He never grew tired of Santa's stories of the many children of the world. Though they were surrounded by the technical advancements of the modern world, there was something timeless and magical about Santa and Mrs. Claus. Having been born and raised here at the North Pole, and having reached adulthood, complete with the same gray hair and beard as the older elves, Scooter had a heart that still resonated youthful enthusiasm, especially during each Christmas season.

The always-businesslike Piotr, forever sporting his plaid bow-tie over his red fur-coat, stepped forward. "I've already asked the house staff to prepare for the incoming storm. So once they've landed, we should immediately head back to safety."

Knowing nods responded to the Chief of Staff's words.

"There they are!"

Scooter lifted his head back up, his eyes and ears focused as sharp as a hawk's. There it was—a faint rhythm of familiar jingling bells and a tiny but steady red light.

"They're back!"

The crowd burst into busy activity. Hands went into the air, fingers pointing skyward. The animals began hopping about, and the off-duty reindeer stepped forward in anticipation. It wasn't a long wait. The jingle grew louder and the light grew larger and brighter. Soon, the silhouette of the team could be seen through the red-lit clouds and Scooter could feel his pulse quicken with anticipation. Each year, it was the same routine, but the excitement of Santa's return always felt as fresh as the first time.

"Here they come!"

The team flew over the runway, the large red sleigh trailing behind. Almost immediately, Scooter could catch markings of a rough trip—dents and scratches, even a few puncture holes. They touched down and, heading up the slope of the clearing, came to a sliding stop. Aurora and Imo, the two reindeer immediately behind Rudolph, collapsed to the ground while the others drooped their heads and knelt or squatted. Santa himself lay back in his seat and took a deep breath, exhausted.

The crowd of elves and Mrs. Claus rushed over to attend to them. The forest animals crowded around. Old stalwarts Donner and Blitzen ran in to look over the condition of the exhausted reindeer.

"Santa!" several of the elves cried. "Are you all right?"

Scooter stared at the sight in shock. Santa slumped in his chair, a dazed expression on his face. The reindeer looked as if they had returned from a war and the classic, red sleigh—the apple of Scooter's eye—looked like a battered wreck.

Mrs. Claus clambered into the creaking sleigh, next to Santa and, taking a thick blanket from one of the elves, wrapped and cradled him. "Are you hurt? What happened?"

Santa gazed at her and shook his head. "We're

fine, dear. A little tired, but we made it back ahead of the storm."

"We must check you over...."

"Oh no, little woman!"

Seeing Santa push himself up in his seat, Scooter's spirits lifted a little.

"I'm fine," Santa insisted. "Good as gold." Another deep sigh and he collapsed back in his seat.

Scooter had never seen Santa like this before and he couldn't help but note a resemblance between Santa's exhaustion and his reindeers'.

"No, I want Dr. Olaf to be sure of that." Mrs. Claus took Santa's hand and patted it.

"Bah!"

"Now dear, don't be a Scrooge."

"Excuse me." It was Piotr. "We must hurry back before the storm hits."

"Yes," Mrs. Claus agreed. "We must."

Hearing this, Scooter immediately ran forward to help unhitch the poor reindeer. Aurora and Imo remained sprawled on the ground, still too worn out to stand. Scooter paused at the sight of the two helpless deer, touched by how they had obviously given the ride everything they had. While he carefully coaxed the two of them to their feet, Serge loaded the rest of the team onto the carrier sled.

"That's right." Scooter supported Aurora's body while she steadied her legs. After Imo also rose to his feet, Scooter put his arms around their necks and led them forward. "One foot in front of the other.

Almost there."

Once they were aboard the carrier and lying down and resting, Scooter signaled the driver to head back to the barn. Serge then restarted the snowmobile and headed away with Piotr while the mighty Donner and Blitzen pulled the sleigh with Santa and Mrs. Claus still together inside back to the castle. The crowd dispersed and as he refastened his cross-country skis for the short walk back, Scooter paused to ponder the moment, deeply disturbed by what had just transpired.

Everyone knew that the modern world could be a dangerous one. But Scooter had never seen it hit this close to home. Not even Santa Claus had been spared.

www.ingramcontent.com/pod-product-compliance
Lightning Source LLC
Chambersburg PA
CBHW020629130626
46552CB00003B/1138